This book belongs to

....

....

....

First published 2020 by Johnny Magory Business. Ballynafagh, Prosperous, Naas, Co. Kildare, Ireland.
ISBN: 978-1-8382152-1-7
Text, Illustrations, Design © 2020 Emma-Jane Leeson
www.JohnnyMagory.com

This book was produced entirely in Ireland (and we're really proud about that!)
Written by Emma-Jane Leeson, Kildare
Edited by Aoife Barrett, Dublin
Illustrated and Designed by Kim Shaw, Kilkenny
Printed by KPS Colour Print, Mayo

Proud Partners of CMRF Crumlin.
2% of the proceeds from the sale of this book will be donated to this charity.
Please visit www.CMRF.org for more information.

Johnny Magory
Joins the Irish Legends

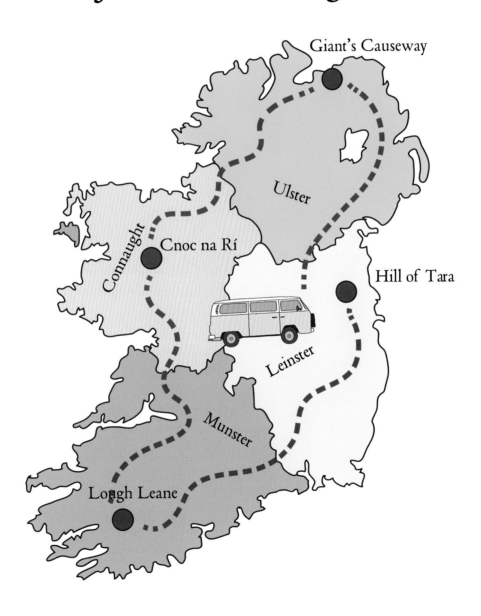

Giant's Causeway

Ulster

Connaught

Cnoc na Rí

Hill of Tara

Leinster

Munster

Lough Leane

Emma-Jane Leeson

*For my funniest friend (by miles) Sean-Óg Moore who,
at the age of 11, co-wrote this book with me. A finer
imagination and storyteller I will never meet. A real
author. Thank you Sean-Óg xx*

*PS. Sean-Óg did lots of research and learned loads
about Irish legends while we were writing.*

Visit <u>www.JohnnyMagory.com</u> to learn even more
about their stories.

I'll tell you a story about Johnny Magory,

His sister Lily-May and their trusty dog Ruairi.

The clever two are six and nine years old,

They're **usually** good

but they're

sometimes

bold!

Everyone knows that Ireland is full of myths, legends and magic places,
A landscape steeped in history with castles, tombs and famous faces.
A holiday on the Emerald Isle is really something like no other,

says Lily-May, packing up Tizzy with her big brother.

"So hurry up!"

They get their map out and make a plan to visit every province in Ireland,
"We'll see Ulster, Connaught, Munster and Leinster," says Johnny. "It'll be grand!"

Now Johnny loves to talk and share made-up stories from his ceann,

But Daddy warns, "No tall tales son, instead we'll learn about each town."

Just before they leave County Kildare, they take a walk by the River Boyne,
Where they see a fisherman ag iascaireacht with a stick and twine.

"Finegas is ainm dom", he smiles at them. "I'm a very wise old man.

I want to catch the Salmon of Knowledge and need some help, if you can?"

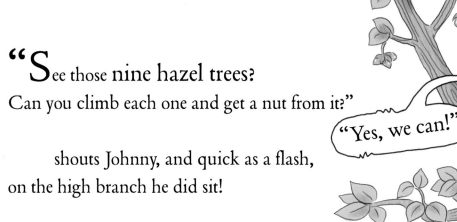

"**S**ee those **nine hazel trees?**
Can you climb each one and get a nut from it?"

"Yes, we can!"

shouts Johnny, and quick as a flash,
on the high branch he did sit!

Finegas smiles,
"These **hazelnuts** held the wisdom of the world
when the Salmon of Knowledge ate them years ago.
Then Fionn MacCumhaill burnt himself,
stuck his thumb in his béal and everything he did know!"

Finegas frowns and looks serious, as he pulls his long, white beard:
"I've an **important** job for you Johnny – to make sure Irish legends are heard.
There's a reward waiting for you if you can complete this mission and succeed,
You'll find it on the Hill of Tara, in the province of Leinster, County Meath."

"When you've heard each legend, you'll get a piece of a wooden jigsaw map,
There's four to collect timpeall na hEireann and Lily-May will help you do that."
Johnny's eyes light up with adventure as he shouts,

"Let's begin!"

"Hup ya booya!"

Lily-May screams,
because she gets to explore with him.

So up to the North of Ireland they go to Ulster
for their first night away from home,
They're eating some toasted marshmallows,
when Johnny gets the feeling
they're
not
alone.

"Tá eagla orm,"

Johnny says, as he looks into the forest
and blinks twice at what he sees,

Fionn MacCumhaill the warrior, with his dogs Bran and Sceóland, is waving from the trees.

F ionn tells them he has built a bridge to Scotland to fight the giant Benandonner,

"But I didn't realise just how GIANT he is and now I think I'm a gonner!"

Lily-May says, "I know what to do! Quick dress up as a baby and get into this pram!"

"You're mad!" Fionn says, shrugging his shoulders, but he goes along with the plan.

When Benandonner arrives Lily-May says, "I'm sorry but Fionn's away,

So ciúnas, le do thoill and don't wake his son or he'll cry all day."

Benandonner's eyes widen; he cannot believe the size of Fionn's baby son,

Terrified, he races back to Scotland, destroying the bridge on his home run.

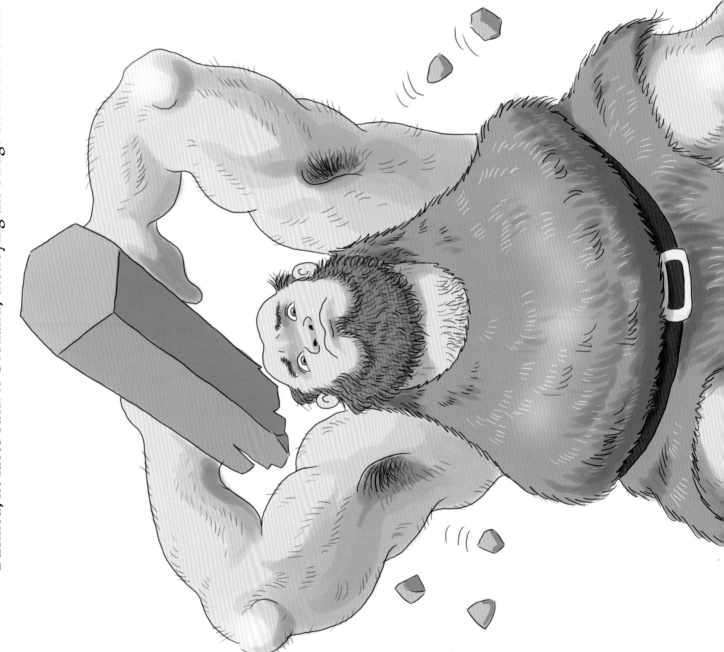

they shout, as Fionn gives them a wooden jigsaw piece of Ulster.

"Now you need to see Queen Medh in Connaught, before you go on to Munster."

"Hurray,"

Next morning Johnny tries to tell his parents about their mission around the nation,

"Whist, Macusla," Mammy says, rolling her eyes at her son's wild imagination.

Driving into Sligo, they see the massive mountain Ben Bulben in the distance.

They camp beside Cnoc na Rí, lighting a cosy fire and eat, sing and dance.

That night Johnny and Lily-May wake up again when they hear a noise,

They look outside and see Queen Medh waving, winking with her green eyes.

Queen Medh tells them about a mighty war, lasting years that started with her husband:

"We argued, wanting to know who had the most money, ainmhithe and land.

Ailill mac Máta had a white-horned bull, something I did not own,

So I wanted Donn Cuailgne, the brown bull of Cooley,

the **best** bull known!"

"Thousands of men died at the

Cattle Raid of Cooley

when both sides did meet,

And the warrior Cuchulainn fought

against us and forced my army to retreat.

But still mo aimn needs to be remembered,

as the greatest Queen in the land!

Here's a jigsaw piece of Connaught, keep it safe in your hand."

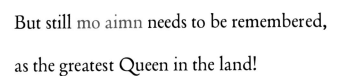

Next morning Johnny tries to tell his parents about their mission around the nation,

"You're a gurrier!" Daddy jokes, rolling his eyes at his son's wild imagination.

Onwards they drive to Munster, spotting seals along the Wild Atlantic Way,

They park Tizzy at Lough Leane in Killarney, County Kerry for night three on holiday.

That night again they hear more noises and can't wait to see who they'll meet,

It's a man ar an gcapall, and a woman with golden hair down to her feet.

"My name is Oisín and this is my wife Niamh Chinn Óir from Tír na nÓg,
The Land of Youth that's under the water, where nobody grows old.
My father was Fionn MacCumhaill,
the leader of the mighty Na Fianna army,
I left when Niamh flew in on
Embarr the magical horse
and asked to marry me."

"Three hundred glorious years we had living in the Land of Youth,

But I missed my family and cairde so badly I came back to my roots.

Niamh told me not to touch the soil, to stay on the horse until my return,

But the girth on my saddle broke when I was trying to do a good turn."

"Irishmen had got so small and weak
since I'd been away.
I was helping them move a boulder
that they'd been fighting all day.

I fell and touched Irish soil, my body got old,
with wrinkles and grey hair.
Three hundred years in a human body
is a bit too hard to bear!"

"Thank you for listening to our story
about the magical Tír na nÓg.
Here's a jigsaw piece of Munster,
for listening to the story that we told."

Next morning Johnny tries to tell his parents about their mission around the nation,

"Ye little rascal,"

they laugh, rolling their eyes at
their son's wild imagination.

The last stop on their holiday is back in Leinster in the county of Meath,
The Hill of Tara where all the past Ard Rí of Ireland used to rule and lead.
The ancient Druids and Tuatha Dé Danann cast so many charms and spells,
The most famous High King was Brian Boru as written in the Book of Kells.

That evening they meet Brian Boru who greets the pair with great delight,
"I hear you've come to tell our stories and a great bronntanas is in sight!"
Brian tells them about his army and all the victories that he won,
His story is full of major battles, and how he was finally overrun.

"A High King of Ireland needs to be crowned and put in place again.
The Lia Fail, the Stone of Destiny, will roar when the **true King** comes to the glen.
And chariots of fire will come to take him to his rightful seat,
The High King of Ireland, an Ard Rí, with the country at his feet."

Brian gives Johnny the Leinster piece of the puzzle, now he has all four,

And as he pushes it into place, the Stone of Destiny begins to roar:

"Johnny Magory, The Boy with the Story! You are the true High King of Ireland."

"Take your seat on the throne," says Brian Boru, bowing and taking his hand.

The **roar** wakes Ma and Da and they come running out, looking around,

They can't believe their son is wearing a
royal cloak and **golden crown**.
And that their daughter is being named **Queen**
and has a crown of diamonds and gold,
Surrounded by Fionn, Finegas, Oisín and Medh
and all the Irish legends,
　　　　brave and **bold**.

They have a big feast and are ag damhsa agus ag canadh until it is bedtime,
Ma and Da carry the kids into Tizzy the van, saying, "We owe you big time!
Tá an-brón orainn, Johnny for not listening - your scéal was all true,
What a **special** storyteller you are. We'll always believe in you."